Dear Reader,

Thank you for selecting *Peanut Butter and Jelly Burritos* as your read! The author aims to spark curiosity and conversation about family, culture, ethnicity, and history.

For Luna and Danny.

This book honors the many efforts of my parents, Steven and Laura Arizaga.

PEANUT BUTTER AND JELLY BURRITOS

Written by Dr. Aryca J. Arizaga Marrón
Illustrated by Paola Jamileth Roman Briceno

Hi there! Everyone calls me Birdie. What is your name?
My name is _____.

I love pink, everything pink!

What is your favorite color?

I live in the southwest.

My town looks like the desert.

It is very hot in the summer.

What does it look like where you live?

Also, México is close to where I live.

My family likes to travel to Mexicali—that's in México.

Sometimes we go to Algodones too.

I try my best to keep up with Spanish, but sometimes people talk too fast.

I really love the tortillas de harina in México!

I love looking at the moon. I think it is beautiful.

My mom says the moon is "luna" in Spanish. Do you enjoy being outdoors?

My best friend is Lisa.

Lisa is my next door neighbor.

We have so much fun together playing

in our neighborhood and riding bikes.

We also have the same birthday!

When is your birthday?

I like my gymnastics class. I can do tricks in my front yard.

I like doing pull-ups at recess too. I even beat all the boys!

What is your favorite activity?

I love my teacher. Her name is Ms. Sidhu.

She makes me feel special and loved.

She gives me a kiss on the cheek before I leave school

Who is your favorite teacher?

I especially love my family.

My Mom and Dad ask me to behave, so I try my best.

My big brothers are okay, but sometimes they tease me.

My big brothers make me peanut butter and jelly burritos after school.

Do you have a favorite after school snack?

Chila is who watches me when my parents work.

She shares a room with me.

I love Chila because we do so many fun activities!

She helps me understand more about being Mexican.

We always sing Spanish songs together. We love songs from Los Bukis.

Sometimes Chila allows me to play with my other best friend, Alexandra.

When Alexandra comes over, Chila makes sopita de huevo for us.

I was so excited to learn about being Mexican, I told Ms. Sidhu the good news!

I said "I am Mexican!" I even said my name in Spanish! I did it!

I told my grandparents that I am Mexican too.

But my grandfather exclaimed "No, you are American!"

My aunts assured me that I am Mexican.

I do not understand!

I asked my mom and dad if I am Mexican and

they made me a peanut butter and jelly burrito.

Yummy, my favorite treat!

My mom and dad told me that I am just like a peanut butter and jelly burrito.

Now I am really confused!

My mom and dad explained to me that just like the tortillas de harina that I love,

our families came from México.

And just like the yummy peanut butter and jelly, I am American.

I asked my mom and dad if I am both Mexican and American.

"Yes, you are both!" they enthusiastically said.

So, I finished my peanut butter and jelly burrito as a Mexican-American.

Have you ever wondered where your family is from?

When you find out, write it here:

I am _____.

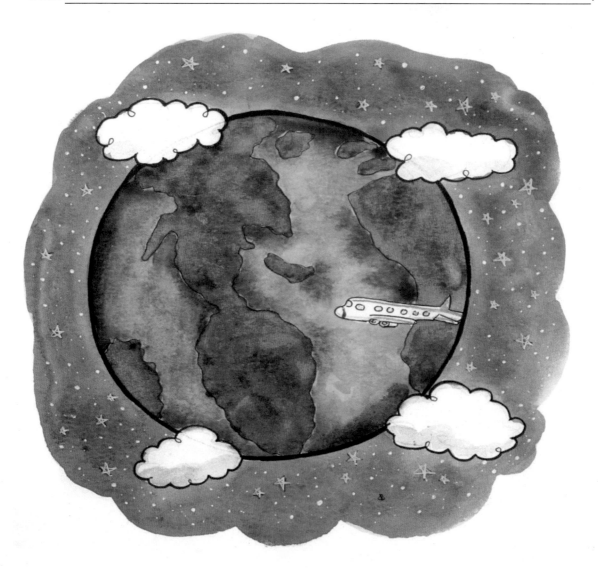

Photo by Ernest Yates

About the Author

Dr. Aryca J. Arizaga Marrón, BS, MS, MEd, EdD grew up on the Arizona/California/México Southwest Border. She has taught for 20 years at the preschool, high school, community college, and university levels. She is interested in human development, the family, home economy, health, and social issues. She enjoys serving the Lord and spending time with her husband, daughter, and extended family.

Photo by Ernest Yates

About the Illustrator

Paola Jamileth Roman Briceno was raised in México for most of her childhood. At eleven years of age, she moved to the United States and started to learn English. She had always enjoyed drawing and taking art classes as a child. When she was fourteen, she decided she wanted to become an illustrator and began to take art more seriously. She is currently pursuing her Illustration and Design degree.

Made in the USA
Monee, IL
17 February 2022

91393064R00017